COMFORT AND EMOTION

BY

NATALIE CLARK, EMILY GROFF
ISA PAGANA, MELODY PHA, &
ADAHLEE SCHROEDER

CAMP HILL, PENNSYLVANIA

For those who dare to love.

THE STATUE
BY ISA PAGANA

Pale, perfect sculpture
Invincible as a Greek legend with your careless
Stance, arrogant alabaster smirk,
Not a plate of armor
Protecting your naked heart.

In earnest I must preserve your surface
Though you make this feat challenging
Being that I'm the bearer of tragedy
You are no exception;
None are immune to this cursed destruction.

I will warn you, drain every meek ounce of sanity
To protect you, if you'll let me.
Or I can kiss you until our mouths dry up
Our minds slow to a stop
And our chests erupt.

Temptation tells me to tip you off that pedestal;
Shatter this fragile
Masterpiece beyond repair.
In time you may put yourself back together,
Losing pieces in the process.

Your pure, untouched innocence will be riddled
With scars—the evidence of my touch.
Are you sure, reckless hero,
That you want my hands upon
Your open glass love?

Like youth with flitting fingers
Unwilling, too long, to linger
Itching, longing from afar
Restless, peering at the art
Created for experiencing.

I must be still and behaved upon your gaze
My muse, my centerpiece display
I must freeze beneath the timeless marble
Silken shadow of your silhouette.

Dare me to graze you, freshly cut
Trace the curvature of your frame
Porcelain, priceless, sunlit shapes
I can almost taste, but cannot touch.

KILLING TIME
BY ISA PAGANA

I doubt he even has a plan,
But I stay up anyhow.
What's an hour to lose?
In the grand scheme of things,
It won't make much of a difference.

There I am again,
Thinking,
What's one life to lose?
In the grand scheme of things,
Do I really make a difference?

Although he doesn't have a plan,
We both know I'll stay awake for him.
I've got an hour to lose.
In the grand scheme of things,
At least to him, it makes a difference.

I'll do this tonight and time again.
Sure, I could lose an hour of sleep,
But I cannot lose him.
In the grand scheme of things,
An hour makes all the difference.

GOODBYE
BY ADAHLEE SCHROEDER

Salt-crusted skin, warm under the blinding sun, was washed by an incoming wave. The soft white of her chiton floated in the water. His hardened face held fast in her memory. Every wizened mark was painted in fine detail.

The soul-crushing anger she could never save him from glared at her.

Brushing away the tear that fell from her eyes to her dark cheeks, the goddess turned her back on what could have been. His raft had already disappeared from the horizon. The sight of it vanished hours ago.

Building that raft had been the only solace he'd had over the past seven years; she realized that now. The sun had begun to set. She began to climb out of the water. The crash of the waves deafened her to the dripping of her sodden clothes, hungry waves pulling at her to return to their depths. If only, she thought.

Not that she would die; death was a feeling she would never experience. He would, though. Almost against her will, her head turned back in the direction he'd gone. A thousand arrows from Eros could not have been more painful.

Rough sand scraped against her feet, the grit sticking to her skin. As she struggled along the beach, Her long thin braids fell into her face. She tripped, collapsing to her knees. Pure agony poured from her eyes and her heart beat itself. She couldn't breathe. She couldn't think.
Raw, she screamed, "WHY DID YOU LEAVE ME? WHY?"

She could see his face. She could see it. She knew he didn't love her. She knew. She knew… But she didn't. Why? What was the point of it all? This cruel game Zeus played had broken both of them. But Odysseus's longing for Penelope would only last a few decades. Her love for him would remain for millennia. The king of Olympus was a monstrous creature.

Her eyes burned with unspoken anger. This was going too far. The wind rustled against her damp form, chilling her. She stood, the tears drying for now. She walked back to her home. What if the gods were watching, mocking her misery? She would not dignify them with her piteous wailing any longer. They didn't deserve that. They stole him from her. Snatched him away like some petty thief.

Her wooden door creaked as she pushed it open to reveal a dark home. He did not love her then, but maybe he would have. He would have grown to care for her over time. She would have gotten through to him. If she had been able to, he might have stayed… She was alone. His cup sat on her table. The wooden surface was delicately carved with no imperfections. Why would there be? He made it himself, the fifth year there. It was then that he'd given up. His raft had sat abandoned by the beaches, and she'd thought that maybe she'd won. But then came the silence. Somehow, more deafening than when she was alone. The silence that fell on Odysseus stripped every drop of hope from his eyes. He walked about like a dead man.

Her hand brushed the top of the cup, the grooves of the wood rough against her skin. Back then he no longer looked toward the horizon, instead he only stared off into the distance.

"I hear them screaming," he'd once told her.

She swung her hand toward the cup, striking it and flinging it across her stone table. It clattered to the floor, splashing water all around her. The resounding emptiness that filled her home bore deeply into her soul.

She breathed in and out. Salty droplets fell from her eyes. He was gone and she didn't know what to do.

TECHNOLOGY
BY ADAHLEE SCHROEDER

"It's smart" they say
"It'll make life easier"

Protect yourself
Know your password
Keep it close

But not too close
Passwords change
That one month
Each year my heart
Dreads the words
"Time to change your password"

Under my fingers,
The plastic keys
Play the empty notes
Creating a new phrase
A phrase only I know,
One that I will likely
forget in a week.

Then there's the accounts.
Sign in, Sign up, Sign out

If one doesn't work,
You're screwed.
Wrong account

Everything I try is wrong:
Wrong number.
Wrong page.
Wrong password.

Frustration spills from my lips.
Burning and scalding
The air around me turns acrid
From the poisonous words
Forming in my mouth.
By its sheer value,
My computer escapes my wrath.

If you did not cost so much,
You would have died.
Your tiny little pieces
Scattered on the floor,
Your dusty screen
Shattered and broken.
Oh how I loathe you…

But I sit back in my seat
And try again
And again
And again
Because I need you.

I need your blinding screen,
Show me the world
I need your plastic keys,
Bring my stories to life
I need the void you offer,
Help me escape.

Oh how I love you

Technology
"It'll make life easier"

LOVE UNSEEN
BY MELODY PHA

Why is it hard to say I love you?
Why is it difficult to ask, how are you doing?
Why—
why don't you love me?
Why won't you speak to me?

Why, eyes, can't you see?
Look again, and decide for yourself:

Your love is….
the faum kauv you cook before sunrise
the clothes you insist on paying for
the groceries you buy for my apartment
the worrisome phone calls while I'm away
the $100 you slip into my hand—just because
the question: *is your car still running okay?*

I'm sorry for not seeing it sooner
I love you is more than three words
that end in a sentence—
it continues,
day by day
It's a choice you make
because you love me

Loving the Old House on Juxon Street
By Natalie Clark

The outside of my house is a perfect example of the idiom: "Looks can be deceiving." Its exterior is charming and quaint, but a lack of upkeep has rendered the inside quite run-down. Like most houses in Oxford, it is old - really old. You can see light through a crack in the front door. The carpet has gouges and holes. When I first arrive, a layer of dust has to be wiped off every surface. The stove doesn't have a handle.

But someone who lived here before us left a bundle of lavender on the kitchen windowsill. And the view from each window in my bedroom is so classically "England" that I can't help but smile when I look out. There are books on a shelf in the living room (which is also the dining room), left there by former residents. Two copies of a book written by Joe Biden sit next to a history of England, which sits next to *Jude the Obscure*. The shelf above holds a glass bowl with a party hat inside. I wear the party hat on my 21st birthday, two weeks after I arrive in a foreign country, with friends I barely know. My bedroom sits at the opposite end of the row house from the front door. It's small, but not too small. Though, as someone who is not claustrophobic, small spaces always felt cozy and safe to me.

After an exhausting tutorial, a grocery run (made exhausting by my lack of a car), or an evening out, I turn onto Juxon Street and feel at home. The short path through the walled-in front yard of the row house leads to a red door. Red doors have long symbolized safety, and this door is no different. I am in a city almost 4,000 miles from anyone I know, but my house on Juxon Street is my refuge.

Birthday Candles
By Natalie Clark

Time to make a wish,
They say, peering at me with
Eyes reflecting candle flames.

My eyes close,
The words already formed in my mind.
I wish to find true love.

Thinking back, I wonder
If other kids wished the same.

Time to make a wish,
I say, the clock blinking from 11:10
To 11:11.

My eyes close,
The words already formed in my mind.
I wish to find true love.

I find him,
In beautiful bits and pieces
Merging to form a mosaic.

On a breezy December day,
Outside the movie theater,
He tells me he loves me.

Time to make a wish.
The birthday candles are in front of me,
The clock blinks from 11:10 to 11:11,
But I don't wish to find true love.
I wish for this true love to last.

THE SKIN I LOST
BY EMILY GROFF

I remember our days together as little girls
when we ran through fields, dreamed of boys,
and fell off bikes–scraping our skin.
My favorite days spent in Canada because we got to go
raft on Sharbot lake as the boat pulled us away.
We talked each night in bed, describing everything we did.

We got older and you asked for new rooms. Why you did
this, I never knew. New rooms meant we were no longer
little girls.
I didn't like the idea of living down the hall away
from you. I fought this and mom said, "oh boy,"
not sure how to tell me you wanted me to go
as she knew it would get under my skin.

You would tell me I need thicker skin
when I got upset over things people did.
But it was always hard to let go
of the cruel things said by dumb high school girls
and even dumber high school boys–
but you were always there to send them away.

When high school ended, you moved away
to college. The idea of this made my skin
crawl. I tried to replace your absence with a boy.
It worked. You asked me to visit and I never did.
You were angry at this and called me a stupid girl
saying, "You clearly weren't sad to see me go."

When I arrived at college, I let that boy go.
He never liked how close we were so I sent him away.
He also didn't like tattoos so being petty girls,
we made sure that we would ink our skin.
We no longer had someone commenting on everything we did
together. We could never be stopped again by a boy.

But that didn't last long because you found your forever boy
that you were going to marry. You would move and go
for real this time. I liked this boy. He never did
anything wrong but I didn't like that he would be taking you
away.
The idea of you gone made me jump out of my skin—
it made it official that we were no longer little girls.

I like this boy, but don't let him take you away.
If you'd go, I'd lose my other half—my other skin.
Because I want to forever stay little girls, you can't say, "I do."

CARDINAL

BY EMILY GROFF

I glance out the window,
to find a remarkable creature taking its perch—
feathers point straight up off its head.
A face framed black with the body a deep red,
Its head bobs, eating from a feeder that once was yours.
I stare in awe at this bird that reminds me of you.
It's color, your favorite,
and feathers messy, just like your hair.

Inching closer, quiet as ever
to not disturb such a wonderful creature.
Nose pressed against the window,
so close my breath fogs up the glass.
I wipe away the barrier between us to find eyes locked on mine,
but those eyes aren't yours, yet all I can see is you
with eyes full of love, fun, and care.
With a blink, a bird's eye once again.

With little food left, time with you runs scarce.
My opened mouth shouts "don't leave"
but your wings spread wide, as you fly high.
Once so close, but now so far.

I wait for you to return, but you never do,
for it's just a cardinal, it couldn't really be you.
But a whisper so silent rings in my ear,
"Sweet grandchild, a cardinal is how I'll come back to you.

FOR THE ONE I CALL SISTER
BY EMILY GROFF

I have you on my mind, my greatest friend
as you're the one I call my dear sister.
You are the one on which I most depend.

My eyes grow brighter from letters you send.
With you around, I don't need no mister.
I have you on my mind, my greatest friend.

I would get hurt, but you always tended
the scratches, the stitches, and my blisters.
You are the one on which I most depend.

My head is full with the kindness you lend,
When apart, I think "I surely miss her."
I have you on my mind, my greatest friend.

I rely on you, you always defend-
Always pulling me out of the twister.
You are the one on which I most depend.

Your love for me, I can't quite comprehend.
I hope my love for you does glister.
I have you on my mind, my greatest friend.
You are the one on which I most depend.

Daddy Daughter Dance
By Emily Groff

As a little girl I wanted the chance,
to have daddy daughter dates with my dad.
Do you recall the daddy daughter dance?

I never had to ask you in advance
to be together. You were always glad
that your little girl had wanted that chance.

But we grew up and you took a new stance-
was it the work or I that made you mad?
Can't you recall our daddy daughter dance?

We began to move about in a trance,
not having something new to share or add.
I know we never wanted this mischance.

I think of times, and look back in a glance
and despite the few troubles that we've had,
I still recall our daddy daughter dance.

At my wedding that's full of great romance,
I will no longer be sad or feel bad,
as you and I will get another chance
to take part in the daddy daughter dance.

THE BEST ONE A GIRL COULD EVER ASK FOR

BY EMILY GROFF

How does one begin writing a message
to the person who gave their whole life
to you? She lost her physique by
carrying me in her womb. I hear today
"I'm no longer beautiful" in a sad, defeated
voice. But I look at you and I can't see what
you're seeing. How could you ever look in the
mirror and think you're not beautiful? You created
life. You gave me mine. There is nothing
more beautiful in the world than you.

When I was young, you'd wake me up
singing a song with a pair of jeans fresh
out of the dryer. You knew I would never
wear them if they weren't warm. You always
made sure that I was comfortable and felt
my best before each day. Who could ask
for a better mom than that.

Even after a long 8-5, you'd be there for
that long hour of soccer practice. You were
never late and never showed how tired you
were–only how happy you were to be there.
With joy, I'd run to you with my fingers up
after each goal, counting how many I had
 scored and you'd quietly chuckle and tell
me "put your fingers down" –though, I could
see in your eyes that you were proud of me.
Nothing felt better than knowing I had a mom
that was proud.

I had a series of night-terrors every night for months. You could always find me slipping into bed next to you with tears streaming down my face. Instead of sending me back to my own room–knowing you were risking your own sleep-you'd ask me what's wrong and tell me that I was okay because you were there. I'd fall asleep shortly after knowing that I was safe in your arms. I never had night-terrors when I was in bed with you. The villains knew they could never mess with you.

In what felt like only a day later, I became a teenager. You were told, "brace yourself" because teens are difficult and they won't want to hangout with you anymore-but they didn't know you and me. I always chose to be with you over being with my friends. My friends knew how much I loved you. When we'd hang out they'd always ask, "Where's your mom? She should come along. We love your mom!" You never believed that they would say this, but it's true. How could they not love you with your amazing dancing skills and silly mom jokes?

I eventually grew out of being a teenager and made it
to college. It was hard leaving you behind–I'd call
you every night and you would always answer. It was
a rough first year-from feeling lonely with no friends,
to a challenging course load, to being locked out of my
dorm for a week and bug infestations in my room.
You were there for every phone call and every cry.
Little did I know you were losing sleep. Your love for me,
so strong, that my troubles became your own.

You were there for my first everything. The first award,
the first soccer game, the first concert, the first boyfriend,
the first heartbreak. The list could go on forever. I never
had to worry that I would be alone. I could always find
you in the crowd beaming at me-supporting me at every
step of my life. For that I must say thank you. Thank you
for never leaving me. Thank you for being there for every
accomplishment–big or small. Thank you for being the
 best mom–the best one a girl could ever ask for.

www.ingramcontent.com/pod-product-compliance
Lightning Source LLC
Chambersburg PA
CBHW031000310726
48969CB00008B/2419